Ms. Gravity

T A N Y A W E I N B E R G E R

LONGSTREET PRESS

Atlanta, Georgia

Published by
LONGSTREET PRESS, INC.
A subsidiary of Cox Newspapers,
A subsidiary of Cox Enterprises, Inc.
2140 Newmarket Parkway
Suite 118
Marietta, GA 30067

Printed in the United States of America

1st printing 1995

ISBN 1-56352-191-1

For more information about Tanya Weinberger and her animated productions, contact Marina Bryant,
World Events, Inc., 4514 Chamblee Dunwoody Road, Suite 330, Atlanta, GA 30338.

Big thanks to

my talented family, friends, and colleagues

who have contributed to and supported my productions.

Special love and hugs to

my mother,

my sisters, Marina and Nina,

Aunt Tanya,

and the Maxwells.

Ms. Gravity

Not so long ago,
at the end of a road,
in the middle of a grassy field
stood a small stone factory
with one gray door.

Over the door hung a sign.
GRAVITY it said.

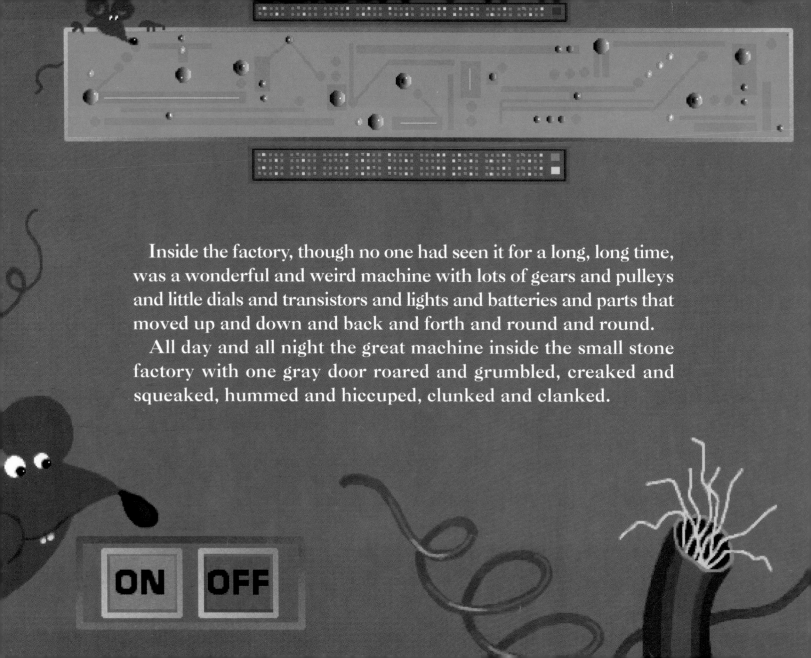

Inside the factory, though no one had seen it for a long, long time, was a wonderful and weird machine with lots of gears and pulleys and little dials and transistors and lights and batteries and parts that moved up and down and back and forth and round and round.

All day and all night the great machine inside the small stone factory with one gray door roared and grumbled, creaked and squeaked, hummed and hiccuped, clunked and clanked.

ON   OFF

Many years ago a small girl came to the end of the road to play in the grassy field around the small stone factory and search for bugs and snakes and butterflies.

Seeing that the gray door was open a crack, and being curious as all children are, she entered.

Instantly the girl fell in love with the great machine that stood in the middle of the room, and she saw that it needed care and repair. She decided to live in the little stone factory and devote her life to polishing, oiling, dusting, tweaking, tinkering, adjusting, and just loving the hard-working machine.

She also decided to give herself a new name in honor of her new responsibilities. "From now on and forever, my name is Ms. Gravity," she announced grandly to the machine, who was very happy with her choice.

Years passed and Ms. Gravity grew older. And, like any human, Ms. Gravity needed food and friendship. So once a week she would walk to the village at the other end of the road. It was a long walk and sometimes all that walking made her feet hurt.

But the villagers thought her strange,
for she did not live her life as they did.
They would not speak to her. They
would not even say hello to her when she
spoke to them. Ms. Gravity believed that
they were all afraid of anyone who was
different and maybe they were
lazy and didn't use their brains.

She could not buy food because she had no money. She ate only what she could grow in her own little garden behind the factory — tomatoes and okra mostly. She didn't really mind eating mostly tomatoes and okra, but she dreamed occasionally of ice cream, potato chips, and Cheddar cheese.

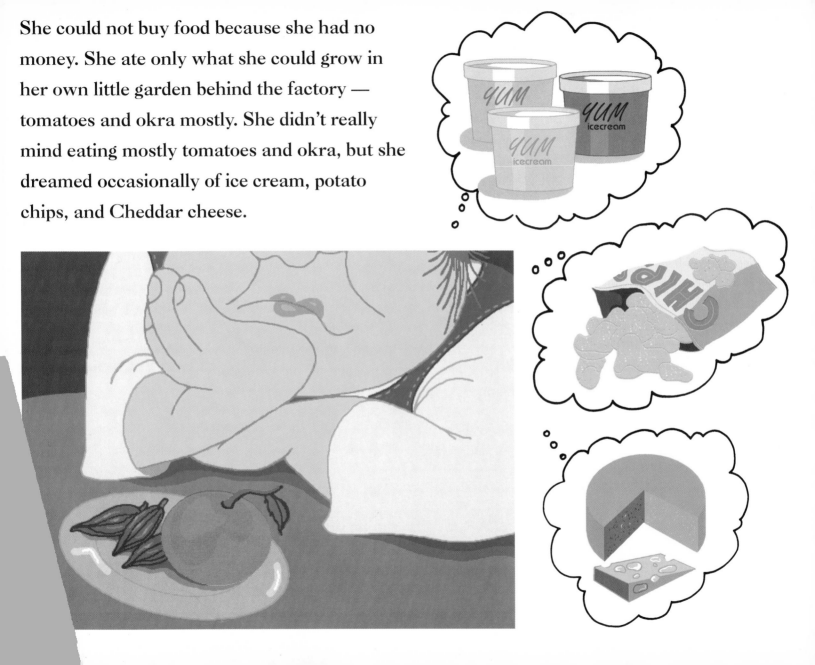

Every week she would go into the grocery store and say to the grocer, "Mr. Grocer, I need some food but I have no money. However, I work very hard every day tending the great machine in the Gravity Factory at the other end of the road. That must be worth something to you and to the other village people. Is my work worth even one pickle today?"

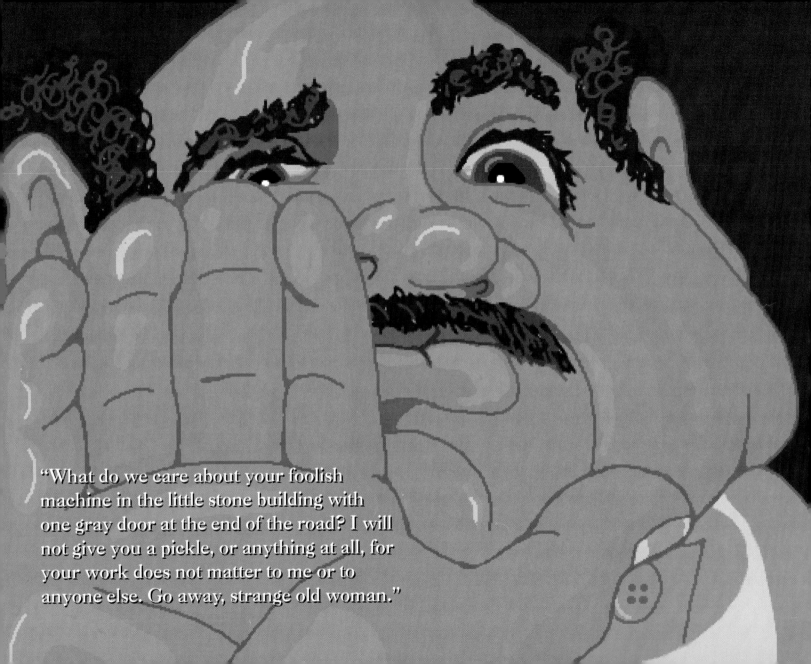

"What do we care about your foolish machine in the little stone building with one gray door at the end of the road? I will not give you a pickle, or anything at all, for your work does not matter to me or to anyone else. Go away, strange old woman."

And Ms. Gravity would return sadly down the long road to the factory and once more eat mostly tomatoes and okra for dinner.

But one beautiful morning she awoke and exclaimed, "Fish! I want fish for dinner." Her lovely machine was happy and running smoothly, so Ms. Gravity decided to go fishing. She closed the little gray door and set out to find a stream with fish in it.

Ms. Gravity had never taken a vacation before.

Realizing that they had the place to themselves, a pair of mice who lived under the floor of the factory came out to play. They danced around the lovely machine as it roared and grumbled, creaked and squeaked, hummed and hiccuped, clunked and clanked.

Without meaning any harm, one of the mice tripped over the machine's cord, and pulled the plug right out of the socket.

The great machine let out a huge groan, then trembled, clanked once, and . . . stopped. The room was silent.

Frightened, the mice ran away.

Night fell.

Ms. Gravity happily toasted her dinner over her campfire under a beautiful starry sky.

And strange things began to happen in the village at the other end of the road.

Morning came.

"Help! Help!" Ms. Gravity heard calls from the sky as she sat peacefully on a pretty striped lawn chair. "Help us get back to earth, Ms. Gravity," the people and animals cried.

She peered up at them in
the sky and sighed.

"Why do you ask me for help? What can I possibly do for you? You did not value the work I did polishing, oiling, dusting, tweaking, tinkering, and adjusting the great machine in the small stone factory with one gray door that sits in the middle of the grassy field at the end of the road. You didn't want to know anything. You weren't even curious. You did not want to be my friends. You don't even like me." Ms. Gravity kept on fishing.

"But we thought it was you who didn't like us because you chose to live at the other end of the road instead of in the village with us. You did not think about things the way we did, so we thought that you thought that what we thought was wrong. And nobody likes to be thought of as wrong."

"You thought *that*?" Ms. Gravity had never thought they would think these thoughts. She looked up at them and asked, "Do you think we can learn to enjoy our differences?"

"Oh, certainly," the villagers cried down to her in unison. "Let's all sit down together and talk so that we can get to know each other better. We see now that you must be very wise indeed, for you are sitting on a pretty striped lawn chair happily fishing for your dinner while we are floating far away into space where it is very cold. We have much to learn from you," they all yelled as loudly as they could, for they were very far away and floating farther every minute.

"Including good manners," added one small girl shyly.

And they all yelled together, "We're sorry. We would really like to know you better and have you for a friend. And please teach us about your wonderful machine and why you love it so."

Ms. Gravity was so happy that she grabbed her basket of fish and rushed back to the factory. Entering the room where her beloved machine sat silently, she instantly saw that the machine had become unplugged.

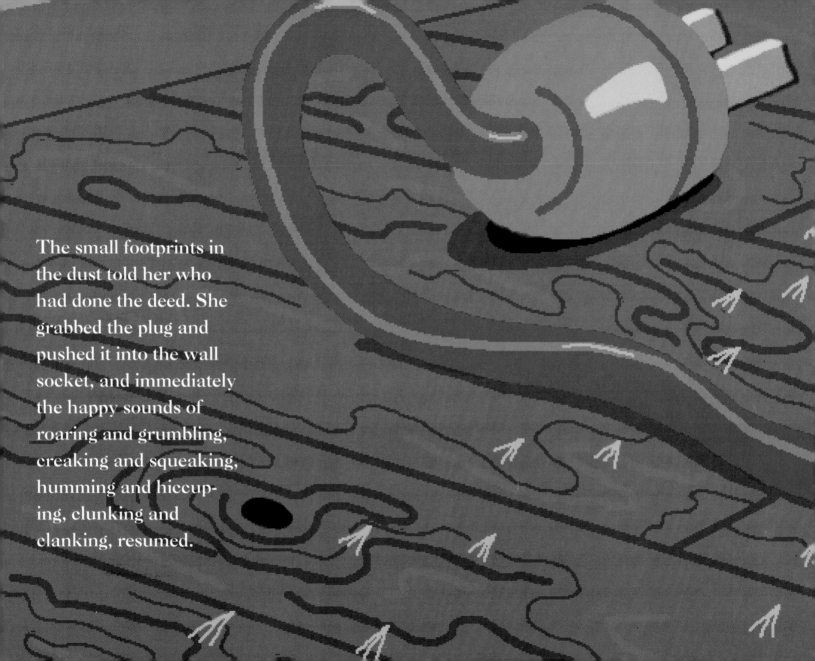

The small footprints in the dust told her who had done the deed. She grabbed the plug and pushed it into the wall socket, and immediately the happy sounds of roaring and grumbling, creaking and squeaking, humming and hiccuping, clunking and clanking, resumed.

And from outside came the noises of great clumps of stuff crashing and bouncing on the ground. Ms. Gravity rushed to the door and looked outside and saw all the villagers and animals and all the other stuff falling back to earth from space into the grassy field around the factory.

The villagers all laughed with joy to be back on earth. They ran up to Ms. Gravity and hugged her gratefully. "Thank you! Thank you!" they cried.

"I have not done anything at all," said Ms. Gravity. "But I am certainly glad that you have returned and wish to be my friends. Would you all like to stay for dinner? I am serving fish with tomatoes and okra."

That night they all
feasted inside the
little factory on fish
and tomatoes and
okra . . . and ice
cream and pickles
and potato chips
and cheeses and
peanut butter and
jelly beans and
apple pie and soda

pop and deviled eggs and weenies and pancakes and pizza and turkey
and watermelon and mashed potatoes and peas and chocolate cake . . .

for the villagers had all brought special food for Ms. Gravity. This was a day for celebration and friendship.

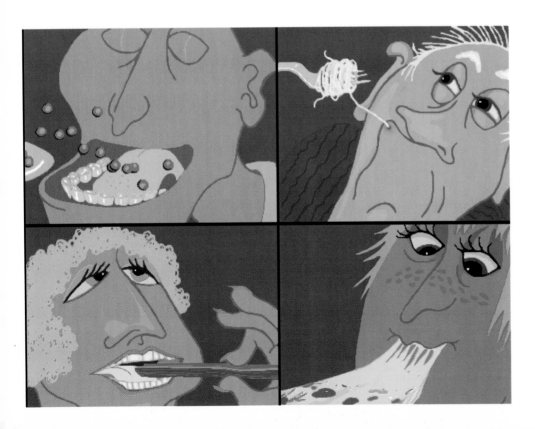

And from that day on, Ms. Gravity got all the food she wanted from the people in the village, for they believed now that she was their friend and that her work in the little factory was very important.

For Ms. Gravity the best surprise of all
came the morning after the feast.
A splendid red motorcycle
sat outside the little gray
door of the factory. On
the gas tank was her
initial — a beautiful
chrome letter G.

She climbed on the splendid red motorcycle and roared
grandly down the road to the village for a . . .

hot fudge sundae.

ABOUT THE AUTHOR

It happens about every half hour. Tanya Weinberger grabs a notebook and starts scribbling, apologizing to her friends for the interruptions — "Wait! I've got an idea!"

She turns those inspired flashes into award-winning films and videos in international, national, and local festivals and competitions, including festivals of Zagreb, Toronto, Hiroshima, Chicago, Prague, and Utrecht. Her works have been shown at the Museum of Modern Art, the Osaka Museum of Computer Graphics, the George Eastman House, and the Boston Museum of Fine Arts. Children everywhere know her work on Nickelodeon, HBO, Calliope, Eureka's Castle, and other cable and network stations.

Tanya and her grand-niece, Brittany

From her beginnings in the animation studios in Hollywood, Tanya moved to the art world of New York City, then to sheep farming in Vermont for ten years, landing finally in Rochester, New York, where she currently produces her animations, books, music, puppets, photography, and paintings with a little teaching and gardening on the side. She draws no lines between work and play, applying her creative magic to entertainment, advertising, education, and industry.

Grace was Tanya's first book; *Ms. Gravity* is her second. New projects include more books based on her most popular animations, a novel and musical stage play, and two new videos, *Ms. Gravity* and *Quake*. And then there's that fat notebook, always looking to the future. . . .